Broken

A Domestic Violence

Dakota Wright

Copyright © 2020 by Dakota Wright

ALL RIGHTS RESERVED. No part of this book may be reproduced or used in any manner without the prior written permission of the copyright owner, except for the use of brief quotations in a book review.

Table of Contents

PROLOGUE

"Shot five times! She might not make it! You need to get here!" I didn't even hang up the phone. The cordless phone slipped from my hand. Everything else in between was a blur. Speeding through red lights, car horns honking, I didn't care, tears burning, blinding me. How did this happen? Please don't let her be dead! My legs wobbled when I stepped into the ice cold intensive care unit. She was lying in the hospital bed bandaged like a mummy. I slowed down as I moved closer to the hospital bed. On the verge of gagging from the stench of rubbing alcohol and hospital antiseptic, I held my breath. The plastic tubes and IV lines reminded me of white snakes. Beep! Beep! The hum of the machines made everything real. She looked like she was in a deep sleep. Stethoscopes, scrubs, and rapid fire conversations increased my devastation. I'll never forgive myself if she don't wake up.

CHAPTER 1

He's Mines May 1995

"Why don't we set it off and have our own private party before tonight?" I was chilling at my cousin Shay's house. It was me and her boyfriend Eric relaxing in their living room while Montell Jordan's song, *This Is How We Do It,* flowed through the speakers.

"I'm down. Let me roll up one!" Eric grinned.

I ripped off my pink t-shirt.

"Damn April you ain't playing!"

I kept my blue lace bra on. Then I unbuttoned my white shorts and slid them off. I sat next to him on the couch while he fired up the blunt.

He called me the week before asking me to help him plan Shay's birthday party. After hanging up the banners and balloons, I was ready to feel Eric's muscular body next to mines. For six months, we had been heating up the bedroom.

After we smoked, my body was sizzling. I stood up from the couch and did my sexy stroll to the bedroom.

Once inside the bedroom, I could smell incense burning. The queen sized bed swallowed up the room. Loose change and nail polish bottles was spread out on the dresser. I thought to myself, *"Shay need to get it together and clean up her bedroom."* Their bed was unmade, I didn't care I just wanted Eric.

After thirty minutes of non-stop passion, we laid next to each other all sweaty and sticky. I was hoping for round two but then he jumped out the bed saying, "Help me change the sheets!"

When I parked in front of my apartment building, I spotted Tyrone's car. My first thought was, *Damn! I needed time to wash up and soak in the tub before he got his ass home.* We lived in a one bedroom in a four family flat on Shenandoah Ave. Climbing the steps to our 2nd floor apartment, avoiding empty beer cans and cigarette butts, I immediately got frustrated with Tyrone. He still worked at the spice factory. His side hustle was selling dime bags of weed on the side. I made the most money working at the insurance company in downtown St. Louis so I paid most of the bills. Every day I was praying he was gon get his shit together so we could move to Florissant or Ferguson and get away from the South Side. Weed smoke hit my nose as soon as I opened the door and the song, *I Got 5 On It,* blasted from the living room speakers.

"What up baby!" Tyrone yelled over the music. His eyes was half closed and he was still wearing his uniform from the factory.

"Hi babe! I'ma go get ready for Shay's party."

"Nah nah! Come sit down and smoke wit me!"

"Tyrone I'm tired from setting up the party. We gotta get ready!"

"Girl bring your fine ass over here!"

I plopped down on the sofa next to him. He grabbed my waist and pulled me close to him.

"You walking in here and ain't breaking me off. Whas up with that April? For real tho?"

Pretending I was into it I gave him a long hot kiss then I pulled away and said, "Baby let's get dressed, I don't want to be late!" I told him.

"Its like that? Gon then!" he backed away from me.

"Tyrone come on. I got you tonight!"

"Yeah a'wight whatevah!" he said and kept smoking.

I showered and got dressed in thirty minutes. Tyrone was still on the couch.

"Tyrone! Damn! Get dressed!" I reminded him.

"I'm good." He tried to get up from the couch but fell back down. That's when I noticed a half empty 40 ounce bottle of Colt 45 sitting on the end table.

"Tyrone you drunk?"

"I needed a buzz. You know how it is working in that damn factory." After a few minutes, he was able to stand up from the couch and joined me at the door smelling like a beer can, his uniform was even more wrinkled. I rolled my eyes and walked out the door.

We made it to Shay's apartment before she got there. Ten minutes into the party, Tyrone was holding a cup of Hennessy in his hand. Then Shay walked in. She looked like she had been in a fight. Her hair was pulled back into a bun but some of her hair was sticking out on the sides. She was still wearing those damn faded blue scrubs. I was thinking to myself, *damn girl you a Licensed Practical Nurse you need to get some cute pink or yellow scrubs.* I knew I was looking sexy because Eric and some of the other dudes at the party kept checking me out the whole time.

The next morning, Tyrone woke me up. "April wake up we need to talk. I got some shit on my chest."

"I'm sleep Tyrone. We can talk when you get home from work."

"I'm off today remember?"

My sleepy thoughts was, *damn I can't escape this nigga.* Then he pulled the covers back. I sat up ready to slap his ass.

"I love you girl. I was checking out how Eric My heart started racing, "What about Eric?"

"Damn girl I'm tryin to have a heart to heart wit yo ass. Let me finish!"

"Okay!"

"The way Eric hooked that party up for Shay. That shit was real. That got me thinking, I love you April. And I know sometimes I ain't the man you want me to be."

"Tyrone?"

"Will you marry me April?"

I was at a loss for words because my love for Eric was so strong plus I was getting tired of Tyrone. I was hoping he was gon say that he wanted to break up. When he proposed, he became that dude I fell in love with.

"Yes Tyrone. I will marry you!"

When we woke up I cooked breakfast. After we finished eating, I started braiding Tyrone's thick black hair. Then the cordless phone ranged. My heart skipped a beat because I was hoping it was not Eric. My nerves calmed down when I heard Bridgette's voice on the other end. During our senior year at Roosevelt High School, it was Bridgette, Shay, and then me. We hung out every day after school at Imo's pizza on Gravois Ave, putting our dollars and coins together so we could get some of that bomb ass pizza because we would be starving after school. The school lunch tasted like garbage. On the weekends, we'd be at North West Plaza mall during the day and at night we would hit up Saints skating rink.

"You talked to Shay?" was the first thing she asked me. "Girl I called her three times but she didn't' answer." Bridgette sounded worried.

"Maybe her and Eric still sleep." I said

"Or they might be getting it in, know what I mean?" Bridgette laughed.

Bridgette's words pierced my heart and jealousy swelled up in me but I laughed instead. I mean what could I say? Eric was Shay's man, I only had him sometimes.

"I'll call her when I'm done braiding Tyrone's hair." I told Bridgette knowing that I wasn't gonna call Shay today.

"Eric hooked that party up for her. She got a good ass man." Bridgette said

I rolled my eyes.

"Me and Tyrone getting married." I announced so she could stop bragging on Eric and Shay.

"Damn April, that's good! It's time for that cause y'all been living together for two years now."

"Thank you girl!" I said rolling my eyes at her comment.

"I gotta go my son yelling he hear the bomb pop man driving down the street."

I was happy to hang up with her because I did not want to hear about Shay and Eric. Plus Bridgette could never keep a man, she had the nerve to say it's about time me and Tyrone get married.

CHAPTER 2

The Beat Down

66Surprise!" All of our friends were piled up in the compact living room. Then they screamed "Happy Birthday!" I smiled but on the inside I wanted to cry a river. My body ached from my shoulders down to my foot soles. I just worked a 12 hour shift at the nursing home.

"You likc it baby?" Eric hugged me from behind. I noticed balloons filling up the ceiling and a pink and white "*Happy Birthday*" banner.

"Yeah Sweetie I love it!" I had to strain my face muscles to muster up a smile.

Pizza boxes were stacked on the counter. My apartment reeked of hot wings and pizza mixed with weed smoke. Eric held my hand walking me to the kitchen.

Bags of ice was sitting in the sink. I was relieved that Eric made me a plate of food. An hour later April and Tyrone finally caught up with me and Eric.

"Girl me and Tyrone we out!" April was a slim red bone. She was wearing a blue jean mini skirt and a white crop knitted shirt. Her dark brown hair was cut into a swinging bob with bangs that kept falling over her left eye. I hugged her.

"Thank you for the party cousin!" I told her.

"Anything for you girl. I'll call you tomorrow." she said.

"Drive safe. Bye Tyrone!" I noticed that Tyrone was high as a kite. My baby Eric was the same cocoa brown as Tyrone except Eric had soft brown eyes and dimples in both cheeks when he smiled. My baby played football in High school and he still kept his 5'10 frame in shape.

Tyrone was a smooth cocoa brown dude with a slim build. He was 6'1 with muscular arms and legs.

"Happy birthday Shay Shay!" Tyrone said.

After April and Tyrone left, Bridgette, my best friend since High School, pulled herself away from a card game and hugged me.

"Girl I'm headed out too. My grandma gon keep Jalen for only so long."

"Thanks for coming Bridgette!" I told her.

Everybody else started leaving. I was relieved because all I wanted to do was soak in the tub and crawl into my bed.

When everybody was gone I started cleaning up the kitchen, shoving left over food in the refrigerator and trashing empty aluminum food trays in the trash bag.

"Let me help you baby." Eric said taking the trash bag from me. "Go to bed its late." He said.

"Nah I want to get this done. Plus I want to be next to you." I smiled at him then he pecked me on the lips. "I wish my brother was here. He would have loved the party." I said.

My brother Ricky was in the Marines and he was deployed to Iraq the previous year.

"You know what?" Eric asked I sensed he was agitated.

"What babe?" I asked him while ripping open the bag of ice and dumping it into the sink.

"Yo ass is ungrateful." His voice was full of venom.

"I was just saying….." I almost lost my balance from the hard slap Eric gave me.

I cried, "Why?" then he yanked me by the neck and pushed me up against the refrigerator.

"I bust my ass to hook this shit up for you and you bring somebody else up?" he yelled.

"Eric I'm sorry!" My face was stinging from the slapped he just gave me. He pulled my hair and dragged me into the living room. After pushing me down onto the carpet he kneeled down next to me and started punching me in my stomach and legs.

"Eric I'm sorry!" The punches stopped then he yanked off my scrubs. He shoved the thunder inside my honey pot. After a few minutes he flipped me over to my stomach and I screamed when I felt the thunder penetrate me from behind. I buried my face in the carpet and screamed.

The next morning, the constant ringing from the phone woke me up. Every bone in my body felt broken, I refused to move. Eric moved his legs over mines. Then he kissed me on my neck.

"Good morning sexy."

"Morning Eric." I whispered.

"You want me to cook some breakfast?" he asked.

"I'm not that hungry." I told him.

"You know I'ma take care of you, Shay. I'll run you a bath." He said then rolled out the bed leaving our bedroom.

When the phone rang again for the tenth time, I dragged my body over to the other side of the bed to grab the white cordless phone from the night stand. I knew it was my home girls April or Bridgette calling me.

"Hello!" I picked up on the third ring.

"I heard y'all had a party over there last night. Not one person picked up the damn phone! Put my no good ass son on the phone!" It was Eric's drunk mother.

CHAPTER 3

Back on the block

"What's up? You paged me 9-1-1?" When April paged me, I pulled over and stopped at a pay phone on the corner of Gravois and Jefferson.

"Eric we need to end it!" April was trying to sound tough but her voice was still sexy.

"Why?"

"Come on Eric, I'm afraid."

"Afraid of what April?"

"Getting caught."

"We ain't got caught in all this time April so why you trippin?"

"Eric Tyrone asked me to marry him. We need to do our own thing. Know what I'm saying?"

"I gotta get back on the block." I told her ass and slammed the phone down.

Back on the block, I had sold my fifth stone then Chance, my dog walked up. The big boss Telly who ran the South Side put Chance in charge. Our crew Gangstaz Takin' Over (GTO) set up shop on Blaine and McCree.

"Nigga you back already?"

"I just had to handle some small bidness."

"The fiends is coming out, we rollin tonight dog." After Chance said that, three midnight black large body SUVs turned the corner. I reached for my glock in my waist. The second SUV stopped and the window rolled down slow.

"Danny G!" Chance yelled.

When I heard Chance say, what up to Danny G, I knew it was all good. Danny G was the head gangsta of GTO. He ran the dope game in St. Louis and his name put fear in niggas hearts.

Danny G hung out the window and shouted, "What up souljahs? Y'all holding it down?"

"We makin it happen, big dog!" Chance told him.

Danny G looked over at me and nodded his head, "What it do?"

"We out here grindin' G!"

"Y'all niggas stay up!" Danny G said and leaned back in the SUV his tinted window rolled up. All three of the SUVS drove off.

CHAPTER 4

Ms. Geraldine

Aweek after my birthday party, one evening me and Eric were home watching *New York Undercover*, Eric was lounging on the couch and I was laying on him. When the episode ended I turned towards him and we started kissing. After he rocked my body, I said, "Let's get in the bed."

We crawled under the covers and Eric held me in his arms. We fell into a peaceful sleep then there was a loud knock at the door. Eric didn't wake up right away but the loud knock shook me out of my sleep.

Bam! Bam! "Open up this damn door!" I heard someone yelling in the hallway.

"Eric!" I gave him a gentle nudge.

Bam! Bam! "I know you in there! Open up!" I recognized the voice it was Eric's mother.

Eric opened up his eyes, "Eric the door...I think it's your Mother."

Bam! Bam! I ain't going nowhere! Open up dammit!"

Eric rolled out the bed threw on his jogging pants and grabbed his glock on the dresser. I threw on some shorts and a t-shirt over my underwear. I stood behind Eric. He barely opened the door when his Mother stormed into our apartment.

"Hey Ms. Geraldine." I spoke to her.

She mean mugged me not speaking back. Then she turned to Eric, "You ain't been to see me in months. What the hell wrong with you?"

My nostrils was attacked by the alcohol fumes reeking from her body. She smelled like she bathed in beer.

"Mama what you want?"

Eric's Mother raised her bony hand and smacked him in his face hard. "Nigga don't you raise yo voice to me. I hoe'd out there in them streets sows I can put food on the table and clothes on yo rusty ass!"

"Mama why-----

"Mama my ass lil nigga. I need some money!"

Eric ran to the bedroom and returned to the living room seconds later with a wad of cash. His mother snatched the money from his hands and stuffed it in her bra. She snatched opened the front door leaving without saying a word.

The next day April called me asking if I could hang out.

"What time you picking me up?" I asked her.

"Gimme an hour!" she said.

"Good, I need to find something to wear." I told her.

"A'wight girl see you in a minute!" she said

We hung up then Eric walked into the bedroom.

"What you doing?" Eric asked me sitting on our bed facing me.

"Trying to find something to wear."

"Where you going?" he asked me.

"Northwest Plaza!"

"With who?" he asked

"April!" I told him

"What time y'all leaving?" he asked me.

"She'll be here around 4."

Eric started putting on his Nikes.

"Baby you leaving?" I asked him shocked that he started getting dressed.

"Chance paged me." Then he reached into his pocket and pulled out a stack of bills. He counted out two hundred dollars and handed it to me.

"I love you, Eric!" I kissed him.

"I love you more." He said smiling his cute dimples showing.

CHAPTER 5

It Ain't Over

I was walking down the steps of my apartment building when I spotted Eric climbing up the steps walking towards me. I froze on the second step. Eric stood in front of me. We were silent for a few seconds. My neighbor's music was blasting through the thin walls. Eric's face looked eerie under the dim lights.

"What up sexy?" he greeted me but he wasn't smiling.

"Hey...Hey Eric...Wh...Um." He grabbed me by my neck and slammed me into the wall. I wanted to scream but my breath caught in my throat.

He leaned in close and whispered "You started this shit. I say when it's over April!"

I felt his hand crawl up my skirt. He pushed my panties to the side and put his middle finger in my butterscotch. When he pulled his finger out he put it in his mouth and then he kissed me. Without any words he walked down the steps disappearing from the building.

CHAPTER 6

Birth Control Pills

I was sitting on the toilet and my stomach was churning. When I wiped myself, I notice the tissue was soaked with blood. Eric busted in the bathroom like he always do and caught me staring at the tissue. I threw it in the toilet when I saw him checking me out.

"You not pregnant?" he sounded disappointed.

"No Eric I got my period." I told him pulling up my panties and flushing the toilet.

"Damn….what tha fuck you doing taking pills behind my back Shay? Its been six months and you ain't pregnant yet?"

"I threw my birth control pills away Eric. You was there when I did it!"

"That don't mean shit. Where you hidin' em Shay?"

We were standing in the bathroom face to face.

"I'm going to bed I'm cramping." I held my stomach and walked out of the bathroom. After I crawled under the covers. Eric stormed into the bedroom yanking open the drawers on the dresser. He tossed everything out onto the bedroom floor.

"Eric what are you doing?"

"I'ma find those pills!" he left the bedroom. I got out of bed stepping on the clothes Eric dumped onto the floor. When I reached the living room, Eric was fishing around in my purse. Frustrated he dumped out all the stuff in my purse onto the couch.

"When I find those pills I'ma beat yo ass!"

"Eric I don't have any." I tried telling him. Panic taking over my body. He ignored me and snatched up my car keys from the couch. He opened the front door leaving it wide open, running out of the apartment building to my car. I ran back into the bedroom and threw on a t-shirt and my orange flip flops. I raced outside secretly hoping that Eric drove off in my car instead he had the passenger car door wide open rummaging through the glove box and the middle compartment. Cramping I returned back inside the apartment.

My menstrual cramps seemed to increase into a wild storm with all the drama. Eric stomped back into the apartment slamming the door. He didn't say a word to me he kept walking towards the kitchen. In the kitchen, he opened up all drawers tossing silverware on the kitchen floor.

"Where they at Shay?" he yelled at me from the kitchen.

"I already told you I threw them away!"

"Where in the fuck are the pills? I know yo ass is lying!"

"You keep pressuring me that's why I ain't pregnant damn!"

He was in the living room in a flash. The next thing I know my body was flying across the living room. My back slammed hard against the wall. I crumbled to the floor crying.

"Shut!" he punched me hard in the stomach. "The fuck up!"

Then he pulled my hair dragging me into the bedroom. I started kicking my legs and arms so he picked me up and threw me on the bed. He yanked off my clothes.

Once I was naked, he hit me on my backside like a mother spanks her child. I tried to run but he caught me holding me down yelling, "Lay yo ass down!"

Once he took off all of his clothes he flipped me on my stomach. He punished me with the thunder to my backside. "You gon stop lyin' to me Shay!"

I just laid there crying. When he was done he just fell asleep his body weight crushing me. I felt like I was suffocating. I thought to myself, *it would be better if I was dead.* Eventually, he climbed off me and crawled under the covers grabbing and holding me like I was his teddy bear.

Hours later I felt the bed move. I opened my eyes and the bedroom was pitch black dark. I could hear the shower running in the bathroom. After he finished his shower, he came into the bedroom and turned the light on. I opened my eyes for a second then closed them. After he got dressed he turned off the lights kneeled down to my side of the bed. To my surprise, he gently pulled the covers back from my face.

"I'm going to the block, baby." He kissed me on the cheek "I love you, girl!"

I whispered, "I love you too."

After Eric left, I laid in bed for an hour. When I finally rolled out of bed, all I could feel was sharp pains crashing into my lower stomach. I opened up the bedroom closet and pulled out two duffel bags. For two hours, I took my time packing my personal belongings. I knew Eric wouldn't be home until the next morning because he was out hustling for GTO. After I was done packing I stood in the middle of the living room silent tears running down my cheeks. I grabbed both of my duffel bags and left the apartment.

CHAPTER 7

Two pink lines

I was sitting on the toilet crying my eyes out. I couldn't put down the stick. Two pink lines = pregnant. Tyrone got locked up the day after he asked me to marry him. One night he was riding with his homeboys and the police pulled them over. The police found five pounds of weed and a gun.

A loud knock at the door scared me. I put the pregnancy test back on the sink. "Who is it?"

"Eric!"

I wiped away the tears from my eyes and cheeks. I opened the door then Eric rushed inside my apartment.

"You seen Shay?" he asked worry washed over his face.

"No!"

"When was the last time you talked to her April?" he asked with an attitude.

"Something happened?" I started getting nervous. It wasn't like Shay to disappear like that.

"She ain't been home?" he scream.

"We need to call the police!" I suggested to him.

"All her shit is gone. You ain't lying to me April are you?" Eric asked me desperation in his voice.

"Did she find out about us?" I asked him afraid of the answer.

"I don't know…damn!" he yelled then he reached for the door handle but I stopped him when I grabbed his left arm.

"Eric I have to tell you something."

"Make it quick!" he snapped.

"I'm pregnant!"

"By who?" he asked.

"You!" I told him.

"Why you gotta lay that heavy shit on me now April damn!" he reached into his pocket and pulled out a fat wad of moncy. He peeled off four one hundred dollar bills and handed the money to me. "Here handle yo business!"

"This is a baby I'm talking about Eric not the electric bill!"

"I ain't having no baby wit you plus it could be Tyrone's baby."

"I'm having this baby Eric."

He stuffed the money back into his pocket and said, "You crazier than I thought you was April. If you have that baby, everybody gon find out about us, if its mines."

"So!" I said my eyes getting watery.

"It sound like you on one, April. You act like we hooked up on some love shit. I'm out! I gotta go find my girl!" And he flew out the door.

BROKEN

34

CHAPTER 8

Bridgette

I had been driving all over the city looking for Shay. We shut down shop on the block at four in the morning. When I got home the apartment was empty. I waited to see if she went out to get something to eat then it dawned on me that I didn't see her car parked outside cither. I hit up April and she didn't know shit so the next person was Bridgette. When I pressed the doorbell I felt butterflies in my stomach. I knew in my heart that Shay was inside Bridgette's house. I heard footsteps approaching the front door then I saw the curtain in the window move.

Bridgette opened the door and just stood there with her hand on her hip.

"What do you want?" she asked.

"Damn Bridgette why you gotta be so rude?"

"Let me be clear. What the fuck you want, Eric?"

"I'm looking for Shay?" I told her wishing I could smash her head in the door.

"Nigga I know!" she said crossing her arms. She said rolling her neck.

"Then why…never mind. Is she here?" I asked.

"Naw nigga she ain't here. And don't ask me where cause I ain't telling you." She rolled eyes at me.

"Is she a'wight? I need to talk to her!" I begged.

"Shay told me everything nigga. Now get the fuck off my Grandma's porch!" she yelled at me. I started raging in the inside but I kept my cool.

"Bridgette I ain't here for no static. I just wanna talk to my girl."

"Nigga you is static. Beatin on my friend. Aw yeah she showed me the bruises told me you be beating her ass."

"Come on Bridgette--------"

"Eric get the fuck ghost before I call my cousins!"

I left her porch. As I was getting in my car she yelled, "You better be glad I didn't tell my cousins to get at yo ass when Shay told me that shit, nigga!"

I nodded my head and said, "Yeah Bridgette a'wight!"

BROKEN

38

CHAPTER 9

Caught

Eric ended up coming over later that night. He didn't even bring up the baby situation. When he walked in he pulled me close and started kissing me. My favorite slow song, *Red Light Special by TLC* was playing on the radio. We took the action to my bedroom. Clothes on the floor, we was making our own music. I was on top of Eric grinding it out when I heard something drop. We both froze at the sound. I looked toward the door spotting Bridgette standing there with her hand over her mouth and her purse on the floor.

"Bridgette!" I screamed.

"You foul April. I can't believe yo nasty ass!" Bridgette said. She picked up her purse and ran out of the apartment.

Eric gave my arm a squeezed and said, "She ain't stopping this show. Keep going girl!"

Six months later, I was eight months pregnant. One day, after dropping off my apartment keys to the maintenance dude, I stopped at the Shop n Save at Chippewa Avenue. I moved in with my grandmother the week before. Bridgette stopped talking to me. Eric disappeared too. He stopped answering my pages. I never heard from Shay so I knew Bridgette had told her everything about catching me and Eric together.

My grandmother wrote me a huge grocery list. I was trying to hurry up so I could go home and rest. As my stomach got bigger, I would get tired easily. I parked the shopping cart in front of the ice cream freezer. My baby started kicking so I rubbed my stomach to calm him down.

"April?" I heard a familiar voice. When I looked up it was Tyrone.

My eyes got big, "When did you get out?" I asked my voice shaky.

"I see you been busy." He said his eyes on my belly.

"H..H..How you been?" I asked him. I could feel the heat rising to my cheeks.

"I got parole." He said

"That's good." I said feeling an awkward energy between us.

"Look April I know what's up."

"I waited on you Ty." I confessed to him hoping he fell for it.

"I know about that nigga Eric." He said. His words sent shock waves to my heart.

"How did-----------"

"I hope it was worth it." A pretty petite bi-racial girl with a long ponytail walked up to him grabbing his hand. They both walked away toward the registers.

Embarrassed, I abandoned the cart full of groceries and left out of the store in tears.

December 23, 1995, I was lying in the hospital bed with my legs propped up in stir ups. The nurse measuring my cervix.

"Only four centimeters dilated." The nurse announced. "Just relax and breathe with the contractions, April."

I was home by myself when I went into labor. My grandmother had been in the hospital for two weeks so I was by myself. Five years earlier, my Mom moved to Kansas City with her husband.

"Can you hand me the phone?" I asked the nurse.

She handed me the phone. With shaky fingers, I dialed Bridgette's number.

Bridgette answered on the second ring. "Hello."

"Bridgette please don't hang up. I'm in the hospital and I'm by myself." I cried to her.

"Where's Eric?" she asked. I felt so stupid when she mentioned Eric.

"He stopped coming." A contraction took my breath away

"April!" she yelled.

"I hhhad a contraction."

"Where are you?" she asked

"At Barnes!" another contraction hit me "Aaaagh!"

"I'm on my way." She said then hung up.

Twelve hours later Amir was born. "You wanna hold him?" I asked Bridgette.

"Yes girl. He is so beautiful." Bridgette smiled.

Bridgette took Amir from my arms and held him.

"Thanks for coming girl!" I told her.

"It's cool." She said not taking her eyes off of Amir.

"I don't have anybody. And it's my fault." I confessed.

"Don't trip. I ain't staying away from this cute boy. Wait a minute am I Auntie or Godmother?" she asked.

"You can be both." I told her smiling. Then I said, "Thanks for being my home girl again."

"Is Eric the daddy April?"

"Why you gotta bring him up?"

"Bitch it's too late to run from the truth."

"I know its fuck up. Amir is innocent. He didn't ask to be here." I told her trying to hold back the tears.

"Get some rest, you look like hell." She said then we both laughed.

CHAPTER 10

How you like that?

"Where you takin" me Bridgette?" After leaving Eric, I didn't talk to anybody for months. I moved into a one bedroom in St. Charles, Mo. The only people I did contact was Bridgette and my brother Ricky. It was a sunny bright Saturday afternoon in June. Bridgette picked me up and we was rolling down Arsenal Ave towards South Grand Ave.

"Don't trip!" Bridgette laughed.

"I knew you was gon say that shit, Bridgette." She turned into Tower Grove Park. She parked her car near a green bench.

"Girl this better not be a blind date!" I told her. She started giggling.

After popping her trunk she jumped out the car, I followed her.

She snatched up a huge picnic basket and pointed to a small cooler and two blankets. "Grab those!"

"Girl what is all this? You didn't have to do all this for me." I fussed at her.

"I didn't do nothing really. My Granny cooked all this shit." She said laughing.

We found a tall tree that had lots of shade. I spread the blankets over the grass. People were out enjoying the 82 degree weather. Kids were riding their bikes. I heard a car pull up so I turned. When I turned around towards the street, my blood boiled hotter than fish grease.

"What that bitch doing here?" I asked Bridgette pointing at April as she was getting out of her car.

"Shay!" Bridgette got in my face putting her hands on both of my shoulders. "We gotta talk about the shit that went down."

April walked up to us. "Hey!" she spoke to us in a weak tone.

I didn't speak at first, instead I turned towards the tree. Then I said, "I ain't got nothin' to say to her."

"Shay I was mad as hell at April too. I wanted to kick her ass-------

"So why didn't you?" I asked Bridgette turning my body around to face them both.

"Because we been home girls for too long and we ain't lil girls no more. We women. Women put it out there and that's what we gon do today." Bridgette confessed.

"Ok!" I told Bridgette then I faced April asking her, "What the fuck do you have to say slut?"

"Shay?" Bridgette yelled.

I held up my hand to shut Bridgette up. "We gon be real or what?" me and April locked eyes.

April started crying, "Shay I miss you

"You wasn't thinking about my ass when you was riding" I started grinding my hips, "that d!"

"Shay I'm sorry, I was wrong." April cried.

"You my cousin April, my family. I bet you got pregnant on purpose didn't you bitch?"

"Shay I swear it wasn't like that?" she pleaded fake ass tears pouring down her cheeks.

"You thought you could take Eric away from me. Eric was mines Bitch!" You always thought you was better than me."

"Shay I love you." April cried.

"This yellow bitch always thought she was better than me!" I yelled turning towards Bridgette.

"Come on Shay!" Bridgette begged me.

"Be blind if you want to Bridgette." I said then headed to the cooler.

"I don't know what to say." April said to Bridgette.

"We all need to chill the fuck out!" Bridgette screamed.

I snatched up an ice cold grape Vess soda from the cooler. After opening the can I took a couple of sips then walked back over them. "I'm calm." I told them both.

Bridgette smiled then said, "Good now we can I took the can of soda and splashed the whole can in April's face.

April screamed, "My eyes!" her face was dripping with grape soda. Bridgette ran to the cooler and that's when I started punching April in her head. She grabbed a handful of my hair so I punched her in the stomach. When she hit me in the jaw, I pushed her down to the grass standing over her punching her wherever I could. Bridgette lifted me off of her.

"Lemme go Bridgette, this between me and this nasty bitch!" Bridgette pushed me almost knocking me down to the grass.

"What the fuck? Y'all out here fighting and these white people gon end up calling the damn police!" Bridgette screamed.

"Fuck this shit! Take me home before I kill this ho!" I yelled to Bridgette

April was sitting on the grass her brown hair tangled up and red bruises on her face. "Bridgette I told you this wasn't gon work." She said with tears in her voice.

Me and Bridgette was silent as she drove me home.

"Do he look like him?" I asked Bridgette breaking the silence. We was riding over the Blanchette Bridge.

"Who?" Bridgette asked me taking her eyes off the road for a second.

I turned my head to the window looking over the bridge and at the Missouri river. My heart full of hurt. "Amir! Does Amir look like Eric?" I asked her.

"Yeah he do, he looks like Eric and April." She told me.

CHAPTER 11

Payback

"Where that girl?"

I was visiting my old bird. She lived on the fifth floor of the Cochran projects. We was sitting on an old ass couch in her living room. My Uncle Ruben called me the day before telling me Mama was sick that she wouldn't stop throwing up. I knew she was just having another hang over.

"We ain't together. She burned out!" I said.

"Well good. Now you can get somebody that look halfway decent. She was too black anyway."

That stung. I loved Shay's chocolate silky skin and her curly ebony hair. I missed her so much it hurt. "Mama you need to see a doctor."

"Boy ain't nothin' wrong wit me. Just need a little rest. Why she leave?"

"Mama you need to eat, you getting too skinny!" I told her.

"Don't tell me what to do muthafuckah."

"I'm going down to Big Daddy's to get you some food, Mama."

"I don't want that shit. Just go down to the market and get me some hog head cheese and some crackers."

My pager started beeping, it was Chance. I reached into my pocket and pulled out eight bills. I counted it out, $150 then handed the money to Mama.

"I gotta go Mama." I didn't wait on her to answer, I walked out of the apartment wishing I never came. For eight months, I had been looking for Shay. I replayed the morning I got home from the block and all of her shit was gone except for those orange flip flops with the sunflower on the straps.

Every day I replayed that shit in my head. My mind would switch from the day she left me to the day I gave my heart to her. Shay was the only person in the world who gave me a birthday party. All my Mama did was hit the bottle, hit the streets, and beat me for any excuse. She was never a mother to me. If it wasn't for the other mothers in the Cochran projects, I would've starved to death.

Mama drank every dime she ever made from selling her body on Washington Ave. The welfare checks and food stamps never made it to our apartment. She would grab her check from the mailbox then head straight for the PX for her whiskey.

After I left Mama's apartment, I drove to the Shell gas station on Tucker Ave. I wanted to fill up the tank in case Chance needed me to do a pick up from one of the stash houses. I paid for a Vess fruit punch soda and a full tank of gas. When I stepped outside, I noticed four cats standing at the door like they was waiting on somebody. One cat kept eyeballing me, then I recognized his face. It was Tyrone April's ex-boyfriend.

He stepped up to me, "What up bitch ass nigga?" The other three dudes surrounded me.

"What? I'm supposed to be scared?" I didn't back down.

Tyrone punched me in the jaw then all of them started throwing punches. I got knocked down to the concrete. Tyrone started kicking me in my ribs yelling, "You got my girl pregnant. Kick this niggas ass!" he yelled to his boys.

Then he said, "You like to beat on women hunh? Who getting they ass whupped now?" One of the dudes pulled out his pistol and aimed it at my head.

One of them yelled, "Put that shit away! We ain't tryin' ta get time for this clown ass nigga!"

"Yeah and we don't want no heat from GTO!" Tyrone said. "Let's dip!" he said then he kicked me one last time in the ribs. They all jumped in a jeep and sped down Tucker Ave. Blood was squirting out my mouth spilling onto the concrete. I could barely pick myself up. Holding my ribs, I was able to limp to my ride. My right eye started swelling up as I drove back to the block. When I finally made it, the first thing Chance said was, "Damn fuck happened to you?"

CHAPTER 12

Daddy's Home

One evening I was sitting on my new plush couch in my one bedroom apartment. It was a cool fall evening in September 1996, three months after me and Shay had a fight at the park. My Grandma furnished every room in my apartment. Amir was nine months old. I was holding him trying to get him to fall asleep when I heard a knock at the door.

"Who is it?" I asked

"Eric!"

My heart skipped a beat. Earlier that day, I decided to call his old pager number and put my new house number in. He called me back, we talked, and I gave him my address. I opened the door with my left hand and held on to Amir with my right arm.

"Hey sexy!" he smiled dimples in his cheeks flashing.

"Hey." My knees were weak. He walked into the apartment all bold and sat on the couch.

I asked him, "You wanna hold him?"

He didn't hold out his arms instead he asked, "What you name him?"

"Amir." He then held out his arms to hold Amir. To my surprise, Amir smiled at Eric. I smiled too but inside my head I was thinking, *Yeah Shay I gave him a son, bitch you was with him for two years and couldn't get pregnant. Eric is gonna be mines!*

He held Amir for a few seconds then handed him back to me.

"He's nine months now." I told Eric

"I like your new pad." He said his eyes admiring my furniture.

"Is that all you like?" I asked him.

"You talk to Shay?" he asked. I did not want to hear her name come out of his mouth.

"No! How long can you stay?" I was offended that he asked about her black ass. Six months ago I saw her but I wasn't about to tell him that.

"I gotta get back on the block." he said

"Can't you stay a little longer Eric? Amir will be sleep soon!"

"Nah, I'll holla at you later." Then he stood up to leave.

"Wait a minute!" I told him and I laid Amir inside his playpen.

I put my arms around Eric kissing his lips. My body warmed up all over. He kissed me back but he broke our embrace saying the words I didn't want to hear.

"Later April."

Two weeks later, I parked into the parking lot at my apartment complex. I moved into the Soulard neighborhood because it was quiet and clean. After I turned off the ignition, I got out the car, opened the back door to unhook Amir from his car seat. Holding Amir I grabbed his diaper bag. On my way walking to my door, I heard footsteps behind me. Even though it was five o'clock in the evening and the sun was just going down, I felt a little nervous. I didn't look behind me, instead I started walking faster.

All of a sudden I felt someone squeeze my shoulder. I screamed.

"April it's me, Eric!"

"Damn Eric!" I said turning around to face him.

"Let me get the diaper bag." He said smiling his dimples showing. I couldn't wait to get into my apartment.

I cooked hamburger helper and salad for dinner that night. After we ate dinner, I gave Amir a bath then put him to bed.

Eric sat on the couch watching TV. I flopped down next to him.

"April, I need somewhere to lay low for a while." That evening Christmas came early for me.

"Don't worry I got you. You can stay here." *Finally, I get to have you all the time!* I thought to myself. He picked me up and carried me to my bedroom.

60

CHAPTER 13

I Run This!

I was chilling in April's living room rolling up a blunt one Saturday afternoon, watching a game of basketball. April's Mom flew in from Kansas City to spend time with her and Amir. After I lit the blunt, I hit it a couple of times, laid back on the couch while the weed relaxed my mind. I had to smile because my plan went smooth, it was like taking candy from a baby. The first time I checked out April's new pad, my mind started calculating like a computer.

I knew April's ass was lying when she told me that she hadn't talked to Shay. So I decided to ask her if I could move in. I figured one day Shay would call or knock on the door when April was not home. The way April came at me, I knew she wanted to be down. I also knew that she wanted me to be a father to that baby. Don't get me wrong, I didn't hate Amir but I wasn't tryin' to be his daddy. In my mind, Amir wasn't me and Shay's son so he was nobody to me.

After my buzz was in full effect, I heard a knock at the door. My heart started pounded and I whispered to myself, *this shit working sooner than I thought.*

I didn't even ask who it was, I just opened the door. It was Bridgette standing at the door, a stank look on her face when she saw me. "Where's April?" she started peeking inside the apartment.

"April ain't here." I told her.

"Where's Amir?" she asked frowning at me.

"With his mother!" I told her slamming the door in her face. I sat back down on the couch laughing picking up my blunt, yelling at the closed door, "Stupid bitch how you like that shit?"

CHAPTER 14

Not Me

On Monday, Bridgette called me during my lunch break. "What the hell is wrong wit you, April? You got that fool living up in yo apartment?"

"You can chill. It's only temporary."

"You a dumb bitch." Only Bridgette could call me a dumb bitch and get away with it. Plus she was the only friend I had. "Maybe Shay was right, you wanted him for yo self."

I was speechless.

"You hear me? April you still there?"

"Yeah!" I couldn't hide the aggravation in my voice.

"Why didn't you tell me April?" she asked.

"I know you would trip like you doing now." I explained.

"He beat Shay's ass. She showed me the bruises dummy!"

"Eric ain't never hurt me." Then I remembered when I tried to break up with him, he showed up to my apartment catching me in the hallway as I was leaving to pick Shay up. He slammed me up against the wall and he shoved his finger inside my apricot gushy.

"Yo ass gon get kicked into a wall, April. You'll be calling me when he whup that ass."

"Bridgette I gotta get back to work."

"Wait! Don't leave him alone with Amir."

"Now you really talkin' crazy." I told her.

"April, I don't trust his ass. You know what? Pack Amir's stuff for a couple of days. I'm picking him up from daycare tomorrow."

"Good me and Eric need some time alone."

"I hope you taking something or making his slimy ass wear a rubber cause you gon get pregnant again."

"Damn you right, I didn't think about that."

"You ain't thinkin' bout shit but being in a fairytale with an ass whupper. You always loved his grimy ass didn't you?" she drilled me.

"Whh..What?" I mumbled.

"Don't play fuckin dumb wit me April. You love this fool don't you?"

"I ain't gon lie, I love his dirty draws!"

CHAPTER 15

I Been Searching

Two weeks went by with no Shay knocking on the front door or calling April on the phone. When April left for work, I started looking through her kitchen cabinets, her dresser drawers, and her closets. I knew Shay's information was written on a piece of paper tucked away. Even though shit went down the way it did, Shay and April were first cousins.

When I didn't find anything, I started flipping over furniture, dumping out drawers, I even searched through Amir's stuff. Frustrated I put everything back in its place. I decided to cook dinner because April couldn't cook worth shit. Shay, my baby could outcook her ass any day.

A flashback of me and Shay's first date hit my soul. I had to sit on April's couch and man up before I broke down. For our first date, Shay cooked dinner for me. She decorated the living room with candles and a red and white checkered blanket. Back then Shay didn't have any furniture, I didn't care. I was messed up because my own mother never cooked for me. Shay called it a picnic candlelight dinner.

I missed Shay so much it was driving me crazy. Sometimes when I was making love to April, I would close my eyes and pretend like she was Shay and we was back together making our baby. When I first met April, I was attracted to her. Plus I knew April was a freak. I tested her last year when Shay asked me to help April get some groceries out of the trunk of her car. When April bent over the trunk to grab a grocery bag, I slid my hand under her dress. All she did was smile. The next day when Shay left for work, April was at my door.

The last thing I wanted to do was put a baby in her ass. After sitting for a while thinking about Shay, I went into the kitchen and opened the freezer. The only food that was in the freezer was frozen pizza and a box of banana popsicles.

Later that evening, it was just me and April. Amir was at Bridgette's house. I kept refilling April's wine glass as we ate the meal I cooked. After we finished eating, I fired up a blunt to make sure she was good and tipsy that night. In the bedroom, I make sure I put it on her, I had her screaming my name the whole time.

When she fell asleep, I got to work. First I went through her purse looking for pieces of paper with Shay's phone number or address. With no luck, I grabbed her car keys and went outside to her car searching the glove box, the middle console, and her trunk. Nothing! Frustrated, I punched the hood of her car and yelled, "Damn!"

BROKEN

CHAPTER 16

Finally

When I walked through the door, I smelled onions and steak cooking. I smiled when I spotted Eric setting the kitchen table.

"Damn Eric, you did this for me?" I hugged him.

"I'm taking care of you, girl."

Everyday my love grew stronger for him. Inside my head I was thinking, *Finally! My dream came true!*

In the past, when me and Tyrone would kick it with Shay and Eric my soul would burn with jealousy. Like the time we had a couples day at Six Flags. Eric played games and won two stuffed animals for Shay. He held Shay's hand the whole time we were at the park. Tyrone did not hold my hand not one time while we was at Six Flags. Then it was the time we went to the drive in. It started raining but only drizzling, Eric went to the car got his jacket and begged Shay to get in the car so she wouldn't get soaked.

He handled her like she was a delicate flower. I was her cousin and best friend but I knew I was killing Shay in the looks department. I had long legs, a small waist, and my cup size was a C.

CHAPTER 17

Guess Who's Coming to Dinner?

Two months after leaving April's ass, on a Sunday evening in November 1996, I was cruising around the city waiting on Chance to page me so I could go pick up some bags of weed. I was driving in the Central West End on Waterman Ave when I noticed Ricky, Shay's brother. He was carrying some boxes from a U-Haul truck to this two story house. Then I noticed two kids a boy and a girl run out of the house running up to him. Parking a couple of cars away from the U-Haul, I just watched the scene hoping Shay would pop up. After sitting there an hour watching them, Chance finally paged me to pick up the weed. Driving off, I memorized the address.

For two days, I parked on Ricky's block watching his house and every car that drove down the street. On day two, Shay parked in front of his house in a red four door Corolla. Damn! I couldn't believe it. Shay had a new car. She looked so beautiful wearing a cute ass knitted winter hat. I followed her when she left Ricky's house. It was like she was driving to another state. When her car headed for the huge bridge, I wanted to exit the highway. I'm terrified of two things, bridges and a judge. Sucking it up, I kept going. For a week, I would park outside her apartment building and watch her.

Then one day I got up the nerve to approach her. Two hours earlier, I had drove to her apartment and just sat in my car waiting on her. Shay parked her car popped her trunk and got out carrying two grocery bags. I could hear my heart beating in my ears. She was wearing the same knitted hat and a coat. She went into her apartment leaving her door open. When I stepped out of my car, I looked around and didn't spot any of her neighbors. I went to her trunk snatched up the two grocery bags and closed the trunk shut. Then I tiptoed up to her door.

Walking into her living room holding the grocery bags, I smelled the berry scented plug in Shay loved. She was in the kitchen putting groceries away in her freezer.

"Guess who's coming to dinner?" I said. Shay spun around.

"H-H-How did you find me Eric?" her eyes was full of fear.

"Ain't important." I sat the grocery bags on her kitchen table then I got closer to her. She backed away from me towards the refrigerator.

"Eric please….."

"Baby I just wanna talk!" I told her. "I miss you so much Shay."

Her house phone started ringing in the living room. "I need to get that." She said her voice shaky. She walked towards the living room but darted towards the front door. I snatched her back into the living room and slammed the front door.

"Help! Somebody! Please!" I wrapped my left arm around waist and covered her mouth with my right hand.

"Shay I'm not here to hurt you baby!" Her tears started falling on my hands. "Don't scream baby, I won't hurt you I promise." Then I removed my hand from her mouth and hugged her from behind. "I love you Shyienne!"

I moved my arm from her waist and grabbed her shoulders to turn her around to face me. "Baby please let me talk to you. Please! That's all I wanna do is talk." I begged her.

CHAPTER 18

Get Back

I prepared my mind for a blow to the face but instead, Eric pulled me close to him and wrapped his arms around me holding me tight.

"Shay I'm sorry about everything I ever did to you. I ain't shit without you!"

I pulled away from him and when my eyes landed on his face, my breath caught in my throat. Eric had tears running down his cheeks. I had never seen him cry before.

"Please take me back Shay!" he was crying "It's been so hard. I miss you so much it hurts." I couldn't take it anymore so I hugged him.

"I miss you too!" I confessed.

A few minutes later we were in my bed and I was experiencing pleasure like never before. Eric tasted and caressed every inch of my body. When he entered me, it was pain mixed with pleasure. I hadn't been with anybody for two years since I left him. When pleasure rippled through my body I screamed, "I love you! I love you!"

"Please don't ever leave me Shyienne!" love washed over my body when he said my full name something Eric never did.

"I ain't going nowhere, baby!" I moaned.

I dozed off in his arms after all the passion he put on me. "Shay you sleep?"

"Almost." I said.

"After tonight I know you gon be knocked up." Eric said sliding his finger down my spine. His words hit my soul like a lighting bolt. I was no longer sleepy. I sat up in the bed. Eric rubbed my arm. "You a'wight?" he asked me concern flashed in his eyes.

"Eric I went to see a doctor a month after I left you."

"Everything good?" he asked.

"He asked me if I had been in a car accident or if I experienced any trauma to my stomach. I lied and told him I had been in a car accident."

"So what you sayin Shay?" He sat up in the bed.

"I can never have a baby. I started crying the sobs shaking my body. To my surprise, Eric started crying too. Then he hugged me. "Baby I'm sooo sorry I hurt you. But doctors don't know everything."

"Why you think I could never get pregnant Eric? I told you I wasn't taking birth control pills."

"Baby it's my fault. I won't hurt you. I promise Shay."

"You still want me?" I asked sniffling and wiping the tears from my eyes.

"I don't want nobody else but you Shay. I never loved anybody like I love you girl. You my heart, my world. I never gave up looking for you. I'm never letting you go baby."

CHAPTER 19

The Second Time Around

It was November 1996 when I woke up to my stomach bubbling. I jumped out the bed three times that morning throwing up. The third time, while my head was over the toilet, my throat burning as the food lurched from my stomach, I heard somebody pounding on my front door. All I could do was ignore the person knocking on my door.

"April! April!" It was Bridgette standing at the bathroom door holding a giggling Amir. She let herself in with the spare key I gave her.

I flushed the toilet and stood up walking over to the sink to turn on the cold water. The cold water splashing on my face was soothing. I looked in the mirror disgusted with how I looked. My hair was standing straight up like I had been in a hurricane and my cheeks was beet red.

"You sick?" Bridgette asked.

"Can you keep Amir for one more day?" I asked her crawling back into my bed. My apartment was freezing cold.

"You know I would love to hang out with my little man but April I have to work tonight!"

I started crying. Bridgette sat Amir on the bed and he started crawling to me. Then she sat on the edge of the bed.

"You told me but I didn't listen." I said then I broke down crying.

"Girl what are you talking about?" Bridgette asked.

"I'm pregnant again!" I announced.

"I knew it!"

"Girl I'm two months."

"And where is Eric? You tell him?"

"He won't answer my pages. So then I tried to page him from the pay phone but now his pager number is disconnected.

"I'm not surprised. Hopefully his ass is locked up. Now you gon have two kids by this fool. Don't cry cause he'll be knocking on your door when he need a place to stay." Bridgette said.

Eric had been living with me for two weeks then one day when I came home from work all of his stuff was gone. He threw the extra key I gave him into my mailbox. I cried everyday wishing he would knock on the door or call. All I wanted to do is crawl under my blankets and never get up.

BROKEN

84

CHAPTER 20

Happily Ever After

"I now pronounce you husband and wife. You may kiss the bride." The courthouse judge ordered. Eric and I were at the courthouse. It was December 1996. We were dressed casual. He had on a sweater and some slacks. I wore a dress with boots.

I looked into Eric's honey brown eyes feeling like I was in a dream. Eric started kissing me. The onlookers and the other couples waiting in line to get married, clapped and cheered for us.

"So what are we gonna do tonight?" I asked him

"We going out! I got a surprise for you when we get home." He smiled his dimples showing making my sweet box wet. I loved him with all of my soul. Every minute I rubbed my thumb over my wedding ring to make sure I wasn't dreaming even though I held our marriage certificate in my hand.

Eric pushed the button for the elevator with his left forefinger and held me around my waist with his right arm. The elevator door opened, Bridgette stepped out of the elevator first then April.

"Bridgette! H-H-H Hey!" I spoke to Bridgette ignoring April.

"Y'all got married?" Bridgette asked eyeballing the marriage certificate.

"Yeah we got married." I spoke up. "What you doing here Bridgette?"

"No wonder I haven't heard from you." Bridgette said looking at Eric with disgust. "I came here to drop some papers off for my Granny."

"Okay, I'll call you later." I said.

"You stupid Shay!" Bridgette blurted out.

"Can you stop being a bitch all the time and be happy for me? I asked her.

"Shay he only gonna destroy you!" Bridgette yelled.

"Baby let's go." Eric said pulling me towards the elevator.

"Did he tell you that he was living with April and got her pregnant again?" Bridgette yelled.

"Don't listen to her Shay. This bitch is jealous cause you got a man that love you."

April started crying.

"That ain't my baby Shay!" Eric said.

"Shay he lying. He ain't even a father to Amir!" Bridgette screamed. A small crowd started gathering around us.

"Let's go Shay!" Eric said pulling me towards the elevator doors.

I turned my back on Bridgette stepping into the elevator with Eric.

"A'wight Shay remember who you choose. Don't fuckin' call me or come over my house!" Bridgette screamed as the elevator doors closed.

88

CHAPTER 21

Choices

I wanted to break the news to my brother Ricky in person. Eric stayed at the apartment. Ringing the doorbell, I felt myself shaking on the inside. Ricky opened the door hugging me as my niece and nephew ran to the door screaming excited to see me. Ricky had the same chocolate skin and silky curly black hair like me. I kissed and hugged him.

Picking up my niece she asked, "Will you play Candyland with us Tee Tee?"

"As soon as me and Daddy finish talking, I promise." I smiled at her.

"I know you stayin' for dinner?" Ricky's wife Toni asked me.

"You know it." I laughed "I have to tell y'all something." My hands got sweaty.

"Kids go in the living room." Ricky told my niece and nephew.

"Shay you glowing, whas up?" Toni giggled

Ricky led the way to the kitchen. We sat at the kitchen table. Toni and Ricky sat next to each other across from me.

"Are you pregnant?" Toni asked looking serious. Ricky gave her a "For real" look.

"No it's something else." I said.

"You sick?" Ricky asked concern on his face.

"I got married big bro." I held up my left hand flashing my gold wedding band.

"We didn't know you were dating?" Toni said half smiling and half frowning.

"Who is he? Any why didn't you let him meet us first?" Ricky asked.

"I married Eric." I exhaled after I let the cat out the bag.

"What the fu…." Ricky started to say.

"Shay tell us you playin'?" Toni asked.

"Yeah right. Who is this dude and when is he coming over?" Ricky laughed.

"I married Eric. We got back together and -----------

"Is that why we haven't heard from you?" Ricky asked frowning.

"We was kickin' it starting all over and he asked me to marry him." I said.

"Why would you let him back into your life? How did he find you?" Toni asked.

"Cause she stupid!" Ricky said to Toni.

"Ricky calm down!" Toni told him.

"That was stupid and reckless Shay. You married that clown?" Ricky screamed at me. I was shocked because me and my brother never had a disagreement or an argument.

"Ricky he loves me. Eric has changed." I said.

"Get out!" Ricky stood up almost knocking the kitchen table over.

"Ricky?" Toni cried standing up also.

"You can't be happy for me?" I asked him.

"I'm not gon watch you ruin yo life. You putting my family at risk. Leave my house Shay!" hollered. My niece and nephew tiptoed into the kitchen.

"Go back to the living room!" he ordered the kids.

"I don't have nobody!" I started crying. "You have Toni and the kids!"

"You choose Eric over yourself and I ain't supporting that shit. Get out my house!" he screamed pointing towards the front door.

My soul was crushed like a sand castle. I grabbed my purse from the kitchen table and walked out without looking at Ricky or Toni.

Eric was gone when I returned to the apartment. I jumped into the shower allowing the water to splash my face and soak my hair. Then I let the tears flow. I cried like a baby the tears mixing with the water. When the shower curtain yanked open, I jumped screaming. "Baby whas' wrong?" It was Eric.

"My family turned on me." I cried.

Eric stripped out of his clothes and climbed inside the shower with me. He held me in his arms then kissed my forehead, my cheeks, and my lips. Then he ran his fingers through my thick wet curls. "Baby they jealous cause you have a man that loves you."

"Why can't they be happy for me for us?" I cried

"You don't need them, you got me. I'm your family now." He said with so much love.

We washed up in the shower, rinsed off the soap, and climbed out. Eric dried my hair by wrapping a towel around my head like a turban. Next he dried my body off too then he wrapped the towel around my torso.

Once we were in the bedroom, he told me, "Sit on the bed baby."

He picked up my wide tooth black comb from the dresser, sat behind me and unwrapped the towel from my head. Then he started combing my hair

"Yo husband gon always take care of you." My body relaxed as he combed my hair. He planted small kisses on my shoulder and down my back.

A month later, January 10, 1997 we moved in a one bedroom apartment on the South Side, on Morganford Ave, down the street from our old apartment building. It was a down grade from my beautiful apartment in St. Charles.

"Is that the last of the boxes?" I asked Eric. I was unpacking boxes in the bedroom.

"Yeah and I'm glad. Shit its getting cold ass hell out there." Eric complained.

"I'ma get up wit you later man." Chance, Eric's friend told him. He helped us move.

"I'll holla at you." Eric said. I could hear the front door open then close.

"Baby how long you gon be I'm hungry?" he asked me.

"I'll be done in a minute." I sounded agitated but he ignored me. I had an attitude since day one of packing so that we could move. Eric hated living in St. Charles. I missed my beautiful apartment surrounded by a peaceful and clean community.

We ended up getting Chinese food. I barely ate my food. After Eric finished eating, I watched him roll up a blunt. He took a sip of a 40 ounce of Olde English 800 and said, "After I'm done smoking I'ma tap that."

I stood up from the table, "I'm getting in the shower." I told him. Every day Eric was either getting high or drinking. After we got married, he told me that some of the members of GTO and their leader Danny Gates all got indicted on drug charges. "All I know is selling dope, baby. I only know the streets." He told me one day when I tried to convince him to get a job.

I did not want him touching me. All I wanted was to take a hot shower, fill my nostrils up with the Apple scented Victoria Secret body wash, slid under the quilts then fall asleep.

CHAPTER 22

Amaya

I almost went into premature labor when me and Bridgette stepped off the elevator at the courthouse and spotted Eric holding Shay. *"That ain't my baby!"* I couldn't believe he denied our second baby that we made while we lived together. What really tore at my heart up was, Shay took him back and he married her.

I gave birth to a girl on June 5, 1997, I named her Amaya. A month after Amaya was born my grandmother passed away. I inherited her four bedroom house located in the Central West End and three million dollars. Then I ended up moving out of my one bedroom apartment and into my grandmother's house.

"Keep all those doors locked ya hear me?" My mother fussed at me. We were on the phone one evening.

"Yes Mama I will."

"Did you turn the alarm on?" my Mom asked me.

"Yes Mommy I did. You asked me three times already."

"It's better to be safe baby."

"Can you go another time Mommy? I really need you?" tears was pooling in my eyes.

"April you know I go on this cruise once a year. I have to hang up the captain said we could board. Love you!"

"Love you too." Then I hung up the phone sat on the side of the bed crying my eyes out. The thought of being alone with Amir and Amaya overwhelmed me. Two weeks after Amaya was born I thought I would lose my mind. My mother came to town when my grandmother died to help me with the funeral arrangements. Amir and Amaya demanded all of my time. I missed hanging out with Bridgette. It was crazy because I loved my kids but changing diapers, cooking, cleaning up toys off the floor, waking up in the middle of the night, only getting a few hours of sleep, packing a diaper bag every time we had to leave the house was draining me. Everyday I wished I could turn back the hands of time and swallow down some birth control pills.

CHAPTER 23

Why?

My last client of the day was put into an ambulance and rushed to the hospital. I was working as a LPN for Clearview Home Health Care. Tired of the long hours at the nursing homes I decided to give home health care a chance plus they paid more. Instead of rushing home I decided to take a drive. I needed a break from Eric, we argued every day. He refused to get a job. I paid all the bills, bought groceries, and supported his weed-alcohol habit. The alternator in his car went out so I paid for the repair plus I had to get new tires for my car.

I made a left turn onto Pershing Ave, I spotted April walking up the steps to her grandmother's house. April wasn't paying attention to the cars driving pass. I found a parking spot three houses down from her grandmother's house. Walking up the steps I could hear a child squealing and giggling. The door was open so I peeped through the screen door but the sun blinded me. I reached for the knob and it twisted open, I smiled on the inside.

April was the first person I spotted. We both stared each other down our movements frozen.

"Shay. Hey!" April broke the ice.

I didn't smile. "I came to ----------

Amir now 2 years old ran into the foyer. "Mommy! Mommy!" he looked just like Eric. It felt like a boulder hit my heart.

"Amir!" April picked him up and kissed his cheek. He turned towards me smiled, waved his tiny hand, and said, "Hi!"

I said a weak, "Hi!" to him. I got nauseated watching April hold that beautiful boy that should have been me and Eric's baby.

April told him, "Go find Nanna!" she sat him down on his feet and he took off running.

"What was you sayin?" April asked me.

I smelled Cajun spices and seafood. It was Aunt Yvonne's gumbo, I recognized that smell anywhere.

"Stay the fuck away from my husband." I told her.

"Shay I don't plan on ever seeing Eric."

"Yeah right bitch. If he walked through that door yo clothes would be on the floor." I yelled.

"Why you come over here?" she asked.

"Cause hoes like you don't evah stop."

"Get out!" April screamed.

"I saw the way you was looking at him at the courthouse. Is Amir really his?" I asked to get her mad so that I could give her another beat down.

"You stupid like Bridgette said." She screamed.

"And you a slut bitch." I screamed back at her.

"Hey y'all need to stop it. Che you need to leave." Aunt Yvonne came out of nowhere. She was holding April's baby.

"You need to tell your yellow ass daughter to keep her fuckin legs closed." I yelled at Aunt Yvonne.

"That's it! I'm calling the police!" Aunt Yvonne said.

"Go ahead and call em. You ain't never had me or my brother's back Aunt Yvonne."

"Don't you stand there and disrespect me young lady!" Aunt Yvonne said like she was tough.

"You know your daughter fucked my husband for a whole year behind my back and he's Amir's daddy?" I told her not backing down.

"Eric was not your husband back then Shay." April put her two cents in.

"But he is now slut. Eric is mines. All mines. He married me and not yo yellow ass." I told April venom taking over me.

"I'll always have a part of him Shay. Our two kids."

"You betta watch yo back you trifling spoiled bitch!" I told her then stomped out of their house.

CHAPTER 24

Not the same

"Hurry up! My wife'll be here any minute!"

I jumped out the bed and started ripping the sheets off the bed. After I grabbed the clean sheets out of the closet, I was checking how Monica was taking her time getting dressed. "Come on you gotta go Monica!" I told her.

"Damn Eric it's like that? Can I get a kiss or a hug?" I wanted to slap her ass down to the floor instead I gave her a *"Don't fuck wit me,"* look.

Monica had a smooth cappuccino brown baby face. We met one day when I walked into the apartment building, she was standing at the mailboxes wearing tight jeans that hugged her hips. When she spoke to me, I noticed her candy pink lipstick. I wanted to tongue her down right away. I told her about my wife and she was still down with kicking it sometimes. The best part was Monica didn't work so I had access to that heat anytime.

"I'll call you when I want some." She said. I ignored her and kept putting clean sheets on the bed. I locked the door behind Monica, then hopped in the shower. As I washed up, my mind switched to Shay. I was not digging how she would come home in a bad mood. She didn't even make love to me like she used too. When I did try to put in work on her, she would just lay there or tell me *"Eric I'm tired my body is sore."* I always did my part as a husband, loving her ass and I promised to never lay hands on her. Half the time we had to eat frozen fried chicken dinners or Chinese food. After I showered and got dressed, I ran out to get some weed before she got home from work.

CHAPTER 25

No Matter What!

I came home to an empty apartment. The quiet and peace calmed me down after leaving April's house. My peace didn't last long. Eric walked through the door.

"You just now getting home?" he asked me.

"Yes!" I answered him putting my hands on my hips.

"You didn't tell me you was workin' late?" he had the nerve to question me.

"I saw yo kids today."

He frowned, "My kids?"

"Yes Eric yo kids, you and April's kids!" I hollered.

"You stay away from them bitches----

"April didn't call me Eric, I drove to her house." I told him pacing the living room floor.

"What the fuck for?" he asked.

"You know Aunt Yvonne had the nerve to act like April ain't a slut? That bitch told me to get out!"

"Shay I thought we let go of that shit!"

"I forgave you Eric but I ain't gon ever forget!"

"So you gon keep throwin' shit up in my face?"

I ran up to him and started kissing him with all the passion inside my soul.

We kissed then he bent me over the sofa and filled me up with his chocolate thunder. As he made love to me, he said, "Shay you my wife and I love you. Promise me you won't evah leave me?"

"I promise baby, don't stop, Eric!"

"We gon be together no matter what right Shay?"

"Ooooaaah yes, Eric!"

CHAPTER 26

Pig Pen

"Look at this house. It's a pig pen, April!" Bridgette decided to pop up one Sunday afternoon. Me and the kids were still in our pajamas. Amir was playing with his toys in the living room and Amaya was sleeping in her play pen.

"Bridgette you only got one son. You don't know how hard it is." I explained.

"I don't wanna hear that shit. Yo ass is lazy. Food smashed into the carpet. Girl this house look like a tornado ran through it. Get these dirty diapers in the trash can. It stinks like rotten cabbage in here!"

"Bridgette do you see how big this house is? When Amir sleep, Amaya up touching stuff

"So! Grow yo ass up April. You laid down and had em. So quit whining bitch and handle yo business."

I started crying then Amaya woke up screaming. Amir climbed onto the couch and leaned up against Bridgette.

"I didn't know it was gonna be so hard Bridgette. I love them but taking care of them is drowning me. I don't have a life!"

"When you pushed them out, yo life ended. I'm only telling yo ass because you been my home girl since free lunch at Roosevelt High. You trippin April and I wouldn't be yo friend if I didn't tell you what's up."

"I know and you right." I wiped the tears from my face then lifted Amaya from her playpen. She stopped crying as I held her.

"I know you still got love for that demon sperm donor. But you better stay away from him."

"Don't trip. I ain't seen him and I ain't looking for him."

"And move into a smaller house. Home girl you got cheddar now." We both laughed.

"Where's the phone?" Bridgette asked.

"In the kitchen why?" I frowned.

"Cause I'm calling a cleaning service to come over and clean this house up. Where the checkbook bitch?" she laughed.

"I forgot to tell you, Shay came over a couple of days ago."

"She must have found out you got some bread." Bridgette said.

"She cussed me and my Mama. Came in here calling us yellow bitches."

"Dayuumn!" Bridgette said then she covered Amir's ears.

"Bridgette, she looked frail and skinny like she need a long nap." I don't-------

"I know, I know. Y

"Sound like her ass need a cheeseburger too. You know Eric the demon is terrorizing her ass." Bridgette laughed.

"I miss her." I said.

"She don't miss yo ass."

"Underneath all that static she had a sadness to her that I can't shake, Bridgette. Something's up with her."

"I miss her ass, too but

ou can't stand Eric."

"Can't stand the ground he walk on. He a cut throat ass nigga." Bridgette said.

CHAPTER 27

Struggle Love

I was standing at the refrigerator with the door wide open, trying to decide what I to cook for dinner. It was left over spaghetti, two chicken wings, a stick of butter, and a half gallon of cherry Koolaide. "Eric what do you want for dinner?"

"I need a 40 bring me one." he yelled from the living room couch.

"I don't see any." I yelled back.

He jumped up from the couch and walked into the kitchen. Standing behind me he looked into the fridge.

"Baby I'ma run up to the 7-11 gimme some money." He told me.

"I don't have any money." I said closing the refrigerator door. I walked over to the cabinet pretending that I was looking for something.

"You just got paid yesterday Shay!"

"That money is for the rent Eric."

He walked back into the living room. I grabbed a can of corn and turned back towards the living room. Eric was rummaging through my purse.

"What are you doing?" I snatched my purse from him. He shoved me and I almost fell but I caught my balance.

"Shay! Get the fuck outta my way!" He snatched the purse back from me then turned his back. As I watched him pull out the money from the outside pocket of my purse, I begged him.

"Eric please. I have to pay the rent tomorrow." He ignored me and started counting the small bills. I grabbed his arm.

"Fuck offa me, Shay." He snatched his arm away.

"Eric I don't wanna move again!" So I reached for his arm again trying to snatch the money from his hand.

Wham! Wham! He slapped me hard across my face. Silver stars flashed in my eyes. I held onto my throbbing cheek as Eric stormed out the door.

A week later, an eviction notice was taped outside our door, it read, **Pay Past Due Amount or You will be Evicted!** I ripped the notice off the door. When I opened the front door, Eric was sitting at the kitchen table rolling up a blunt.

"Did you see the eviction notice, Eric?"

I threw the notice on the kitchen table.

"Fuck him he ain't kicking nobody out." Our landlord was old man Samuel. He was a cranky man, too and he was known for kicking people out of their apartments in the middle of January.

"We short a hundred dollars, Eric."

"He'll get it when we give it to him. I don't wanna talk about that shit Shay."

I didn't say anymore. The last thing I wanted to do after work was argue. Plus my back felt like somebody kicked it in with steel combat boots.

Knock! Knock!

I froze and looked over at Eric when I heard taps at the door.

I whispered to Eric, "I think it's him, Eric what we gon do?"

"Don't answer." He whispered back.

Knock! Knock! "Open it before I kick it in!"

Every muscle in my body relaxed when I heard the familiar voice on the other side of the door.

"Boy I know you in there!" it was Eric's drunk Mama.

Eric jumped up from the kitchen table and opened the door.

"You forgot about yo Mama hunh? Nigga I ain't seen you in a year! What she doing here?" she pointed at me like I was a criminal.

"Mama I ain't got no money."

"Nigga I'm yo Mama. I shitted you out. You watch yo black ass mouth!"

"Mama I ain't working right now!"

"Seem like you doing fine to me." She said her eyes roaming around the apartment. She ran her bony wrinkled hand over the sofa. "Mama only need a few chips. You spending all yo money on this thang. How you gon put her black ass over yo own Mama?"

To my surprise, Eric grabbed her skinny arm and said, "Mama you gotta go. Me and my wife got somewhere we need to be."

"Wife!" she snatched her arm away.

"Yeah me and Shay got married." He told her.

"I'm still you Mama and you don't evah put no bitch over me." Eric grabbed her arm again.

"Mama you gotta go."

She moved like the speed of lighting smacking Eric across his face. Then she balled up her skinny fingers into a fist and started punching him in his head. He held his arms over his head to block her blows. "Mama I'm sorry! Mama I'm sorry!"

"I'll tear this muthafuckin house up, if you evah raise up on me." She screamed as she rained punches on his head like it was a punching bag.

"Mama I was trippin! I'm sorry!" Eric said hesitating to move his arms away from his face. His Mama stopped punching, her fist still balled up. She turned towards me breathing fast her chest going up and down. Before she walked out the door, she looked me up and down.

"Gimme some money Shay." Eric's voice was shaky.

"Did you forget we already short on the rent?"

Eric's right hand went for my neck, he squeezed it then slammed me up against the door. "Shyienne! Gimme the muthafuckin money?"

Unable to breathe or speak, I gasped, "In my purse." He snatched the money out of my purse and ran out the door to catch his Mama.

CHAPTER 28

We Back At It!

I couldn't believe my eyes. April was on an escalator going up. I was wit my nigga Shank. He was tryin' to get on as a janitor at one of them fancy buildings downtown. I was standing in the lobby waiting on him to finish his interview and that's when I spotted April.

"April! April! I called out to her.

She turned around smiling then she frowned when she noticed it was me. I ran up the escalator steps until I was standing face to face with her. She was dressed in a light grey skirt suit with a pink silk shirt underneath her suit jacket. The skirt stopped above her knee. My eyes roamed over her legs up to the curve of her butt. The clear lip gloss making her lips shiny and sexy.

"Whas up? How you been?" My palms got sweaty. April was looking delicious.

She folded her arms over her chest, "Now you know me?"

"Why you gotta be like that?" I asked. Every strand of her brown hair was in place. She looked like a model on the cover of Essence magazine.

"Let me refresh your memory. That ain't my baby." She frowned.

I could see through all that tough girl shit. I wanted to taste her lips again and I knew that she missed me too.

"Bridgette put me on blast in front of my wife. What was I supposed to do?"

"Nigga please. You dissed me and yo kids when you left me." she said. I could smell her vanilla perfume.

"Left you. April we was not together like that. You let me chill at yo spot----

"Aw I see you was using me?"

"Did you have a girl or boy?" I asked her. All that noise she was making I wasn't tryin' to hear it.

"A girl."

"What's her name?"

"Amaya."

"Amir and Amaya hunh?" I asked her.

"Eric I gotta go. I need to get to work." She turned to leave.

"Where you work?" I asked her as she was walking away.

"Johnson and Higgins." She yelled not turning around.

"April! Wait I wanna see my kids."

CHAPTER 29

All I Need!

"April you have a call on line one!"

I was sitting at my desk printing out expense reports for the top executives. The last place I wanted to be was at work because the night before Amaya was up with a fever. I barely got any sleep and that morning I was tired as hell. The three million dollars that I inherited from my grandmother, was broken into payments over ten years. Even though I had money coming in I still had to work.

"This is April Reed how can I help you?" I answered after hitting the #1 button.

"This Eric!"

"How did you get my work number?" Hearing his voice, I immediately heated up. All I wanted was to feel him inside me.

"My car broke down can you loan me some bread? You know I'm good for it."

I could hear car horns blowing and people talking in the background. I knew he was at a pay phone.

"How much you need?" I asked him.

"Eight hundred."

"I'll have it for you tomorrow."

"Where can I meet you?" he asked me.

"Meet me here at my job."

"A'wight I'll holla at you then." I heard disappointment in his voice. But I had to keep him away from me. I promised myself and I promised Bridgette.

The next day when he stopped by my job to pick up the money, I met him in the hallway. When I handed him the money, our hands touched electricity shot from my heart and traveled down to my love box, instantly I had to have him. That strong woman shit disappeared. I took him up to the 16th floor, where the entire floor was vacant. A consulting company used to occupy that floor but the company moved months ago.

"I miss you so much baby. Yeah right there!" I moaned. "It feels so good, Eric. Don't stop!" I was bent over a chair.

"Shh girl! Somebody gon hear us!"

"Boy ain't nobody up here! Let me get on top?"

BROKEN

CHAPTER 30

He Really Loves Me

As soon as I opened the front door, I smelled fried chicken and buttered biscuits. Eric set the kitchen table. He smiled at me while lighting the candles.

"Baby what's all this?" Butta Love by Next was playing on the radio.

"Come here!" he held out his arms and hugged me tight. "I got us dinner tonight, yo favorite Popeye's Chicken." He smiled.

"Thank you baby." I said then kissed him.

"Go change your clothes, get comfortable." He smiled his dimples showing.

"Alright." I said and headed towards the bedroom.

"Hold on baby!" he said so I turned around and walked back into the living room.

He reached into his front jean pocket and pulled out a wad of cash. He peeled off $400 and handed it to me. "Here's the rent money." My heart throbbed with love.

After I changed out of my scrubs, we sat down and ate dinner together by candle light. When we were done, Eric ran me a bubble bath. In the tub, I inhaled the bubble gum scented bubble bath and smiled inside out.

CHAPTER 31

You wanna take it there?

I was lying next to Eric. Amaya and Amir were in their beds asleep. We were face to face.

"Why did you marry her?"

"Damn! Why you gotta go there? I ain't come over here to talk about that shit."

"I'm just saying Eric, you married Shay but you here wit me."

"You wanna take it there April?"

I sat up in the bed, "Yeah."

"I love Shay... Fuck it...I wish I can have both of y'all."

"You love me?" I had to know.

"Yes April, I love you girl."

"Look Eric, I want you…..you can have me, baby but promise me its only gon be me and Shay no other girls."

"I'm down with that."

The next morning Eric was kissing my neck.

"I gotta go." He whispered in my ear.

"What time is it?" I asked him rubbing my eyes.

"It's four in the morning, April. Go back to sleep."

"When you coming back?" I rolled over to face him. I started rubbing his arms. He was already dressed.

"I'll call you tomorrow."

"Why tomorrow Eric? Why not tonight? I wanna hear yo sexy ass voice before I go to sleep?"

"You know Shay get home at 3."

"So what you tell her last night?" I asked him.

"I can't be calling you when my wife at home." His words slapped me in the face.

"You remember what I said Eric. Only me and Shay."

"You and Shay is all I need."

"She may be yo wife but I'm yo baby mama!" I told him. He kissed me. Then he asked, "April let me hold $500 dollars."

"Don't trip baby I got you." I slid from under the covers in my birthday suit. I wrote him a check for $800 dollars and handed it to him.

CHAPTER 32

Where you been?

"Eric! Where you been?" as soon as I walked through the front door, Shay was standing in the living room wearing her blue scrubs her hair pulled back into a ponytail. I like it better when she wore her hair flowing not pulled back.

"I was out hustling with Chance, baby." I kissed her on the lips.

I reached into my pocket to give her some cash but then I remembered April wrote me a check. "Damn I must have lost that lighter." I played it off.

"Next time tell me you out hustling. I was worried baby."

"Ain't nothing gon happen to me." I hugged her tight. Shay smelled fresh like Zest soap. I wanted her to wear perfume like April.

"I need to get to work before I'm late."

"I love you." I told her.

"Love you too." She said.

CHAPTER 33

Tomorrow

"Eric its 2am where you going?"

"Home."

"Why?"

"Quit asking me dumb ass questions, April."

"It's been a week since we been together."

"And we ain't gon see each other if my wife find out."

I wanted to scream and rip the sheets off the bed and smack Eric every time he mentioned Shay's name.

"Baby please stay til four." I stood in front of him in my black lace bra and bikini panties blocking the bedroom door.

"I told Shay I was out hustling with Chance."

"So! Hustling ain't like clocking in and out Eric. You can leave when you want to."

"I'll hit you up tomorrow, April." He walked away brushing up against me.

"You coming back tomorrow night, Eric?"

He didn't answer right away he kept walking down the steps. Then he said,

"I'll hit you up tomorrow."

CHAPTER 34

Monica

It was eleven o'clock at night when I got home from work. The muscles in my legs was screaming. I worked a double shift at this new nursing home. With Eric not working, I had to get a part-time job. The apartment was quiet. Eric called me to tell me that he was going to be home late because he was out hustling with Chance. I needed him that night. All I wanted was a hot bubble bath to soothe my aching legs and for him to hold me until I drifted off to sleep. On my way to the bathroom, I heard a knock at the door.

"Who is it?" I asked curious.

"Monica!"

"I don't know a Monica. You got the wrong door."

"Is Eric home?" I heard a different female voice.

I opened the door. It was a crowd of people outside my door. A pregnant girl standing in the middle of the crowd. Her hair was curled in perfect crinkles. Standing next to her was a taller girl, very slim.

"Why you looking for Eric?" I asked both of the girls.

"He hit my sister, where his bitch ass at?" a younger dude, light skin with braids going to the back, walked from the back of the crowd his face twisted in anger.

"You his wife?" the tall thin girl asked.

"Yes!" I answered folding my arms.

"I'm Monica and----- she started crying.

The tall girl spoke up, "Look he got my sister pregnant and smacked her telling her this not his baby!"

I stepped back and slammed the door in their faces.

I called in sick to work the next day. Most of the night I couldn't sleep, so I stayed up waiting for Eric to walk through the door.

"So Monica having your baby?" I fired on his ass as soon as he walked through the door.

"What da fuck, Shay?"

"Eric don't play mind games wit me. She came here with her people."

"Wit her people?"

"Yeah it was about ten of em plus her and her big ass stomach ----- I started crying.

"Baby!" Eric reached out to touch me. I snatched away from him.

"Shay that ain't my baby she lyin."

"Eric did you mess with her?"

"One time but I used a rubber----------

"I knew it! You ain't gon change----------

"Shay baby please that ain't my baby."

"Just like Amir and April's new baby ain't yours?"

"Shay don't leave me please!" tears started rolling down his cheeks. "I only love you. You my heart Shay. The only kids I'm claiming is the shorties we gon have!"

We ended up moving a week later to a one bedroom on Magnolia Ave.

CHAPTER 35

Dingy Yellow Blanket

"Baby come ride wit me."

It was my day off and we were home relaxing until Eric realized he ran out of weed. I was in the living room watching New York Undercover.

"Eric can we go when this goes off?"

"I told Chance twenty minutes, baby!"

"Eric?"

"I'll make it up to you." He kissed me and I melted like butter. We hopped into his navy blue 1985 Buick Regal and he drove downtown to meet Chance. Eric pulled up to this ghetto ass liquor store on Cass and Tucker Ave. Chance was standing outside the liquor store smoking on a cigarillo talking to two other dudes who was sipping on 40s.

Eric hopped out the car. He talked to Chance for a minute then they exchanged weed and money. When Eric opened the driver's door, I heard a female voice. "There my boy. Come here son?" I turned my head toward the noise and I spotted Eric's mother running towards the car. She was wrapped up in a dingy yellow blanket. It was a cold November night and the wind was kicking. Eric froze when he spotted her. Her hair was standing up at attention and she was wearing flip flops, her crusty feet exposed to the icy wind.

"Boy where you been? You forgot you had a Mama?"

"Mama I gotta take Shay home."

She cut her blood shot red eyes at me through the car windshield then looked back at Eric. "Fuck is wrong wit you? I ho'ed out here in these streets just so you could eat. Yo daddy never gave a damn about you!"

"Get in the car Mama. I'ma take you home."

Then a skinny black as tar dude with rotten teeth walked out the store and said to Eric's Mom, "Coco let's go."

"I'ma deal with yo no good ass later." She rolled her eyes at Eric and joined the dude with the rotten teeth. They headed down a dark alley.

Eric was quiet on the way home. I didn't say a word to him. Instead I let him stay in his own world.

CHAPTER 36

Cocoa

My childhood was far from normal. With Geraldine Johnson for a Mama, a nigga didn't have a chance. The only thing that kept me from dying in the streets was football. Seeing my Mama walking around with a nasty ass blanket took me back to the day I turned eight years old.

"Come on let Coco make you feel good Daddy?" I stood out in the hallway of the motel while Mama worked. I was eight years old and it was my birthday. Strangers was walking past and I had nowhere to hide. The manager showed his bitch ass up.

"You can't hang around here boy, now get!" I walked away. It wasn't like I could tell him I was waiting for my Mama to get done tricking. I ended up strolling to the bus stop across the street

from the motel to wait for her. It seemed like forever as the day turned to night, my stomach was growling from not having anything to eat since the day before. All I could do was watch the headlights of the cars speed down Grand Ave. After eight hours of sitting at that bus stop, Mama came looking for me.

"Eric! Eric!" I heard her yelling my name. She was standing in front of the motel swaying back and forth. Her wig crooked like she had been in a wrestling match. I crossed the busy street, cars whizzing by.

"Mama I'm hungry."

"Come...come on let's..let's... her eyes were half closed. "You want some China man?"

A car pulled over to the curb in front of us. "Hey Coco you need a ride?" the man she was doing tricks with leaned over the passenger seat.

Mama grabbed me by the wrist and we hopped into his car. I sat in the back seat. His car had bucket seats and every time he stopped at a red light, I saw him slide his hand up Mama's dress. He dropped us off in front of the Darst Webb projects, where we lived.

"Mama we still getting something to eat?"

She reached into her pursed and pulled out seven crumpled up dollar bills and shoved the bills into my hand. "Here now leave me the hell alone." She headed up to our apartment and left me standing there by myself. I walked to the convenience store that was ten blocks away. My birthday meal was a cold cut sandwhich with bolgna, ham, salami, and a slice of cheese on white bread, a bag of bbq chips, and a grape juice.

148

CHAPTER 37

Throw Down

"You ain't gon hit it then leave, not tonight, Eric."

"April move. I ain't playing wit you girl."

It was 2am in the morning. I was dressed in my turquoise green lace panties and bra blocking Eric from leaving the bedroom door.

"When you gon leave her and be with me Eric?"

Slap! My cheek felt like it was on fire. "You slut." He hissed.

"Fuck you Eric!" I punched him in his jaw, every bone in my knuckles felt cracked.

He held his jaw and then this crazy ass fool started smiling. "You gon get tow out tha frame tonight, bitch!"

I screamed and tried to run but he moved fast like a cheetah snatching me by my waist, lifting me up then slamming me onto the floor.

CHAPTER 38

A Blast from the Past

Some of our stuff was still in moving boxes. On my only day off I decided to start unpacking while Eric was gone. The first box I opened was Eric's clothes. I dumped everything on our bed so I could put his clothes in his drawer. A picture fell out of one his jacket pockets. It was an old picture the kind when you press a button a bright light flashed and the picture slid out of the camera.

Eric was young in the picture. He was smiling standing next to a mocha brown man dressed in a burgundy suit, a fur hat, two gold chains around his neck, and two big rings on each hand. My first thought was, this is Eric's dad.

When he got home later that night, I showed him the picture. He had a faraway look in his eyes as he stared at the picture. "That's David the man that shoulda been my daddy." He threw the picture on top of the dresser and walked away.

CHAPTER 39

David

David was my Mama's pimp. He was smooth, too. One of the coolest cats I ever knew. From the way he rapped to the ladies to the threads he wore on a daily. David kept fat wads of money on him and a fine ass woman on each arm. Women was always standing by his side whenever he had to make a presence around town. I always dreamed of the day when Mama would sit me down and tell me that David was my Pops but it never happened because he was not my biological. I met David when my Moms bought him home. She had been MIA for three days.

Come to find out, she was locked up. The police did a sweep on Washington Ave (the hoe stroll) on the night she was working. She and her prostitute friends was thrown in the paddy wagon. David posted bail for my Moms, her friend Rhonda, and her friend Ruthann. I was sitting in the living room on that old ass couch we had back then watching cartoons on a black and white TV when Mama walked through the door. She acted like she ain't been gon for three days away from her eight year old son. David walked in behind her, then Ruthann and Rhonda. His clothes caught my eye. He had on black slacks and a purple silk shirt. Niggas in the projects didn't dress like that.

"This yo lil man?" he asked my Mama.

"Yeah that's my boy." She said not even looking at me she just kept walking to her bedroom.

"Y'all be ready by seven." He told my Mama and her friends.

"Ready? Shit wit what? David we ain't got no clothes for the job." Ruthann told him. She glanced at me then smiled and said, "I mean party tonight."

"I'ma have everything y'all need but I'ma take it out yo pay." He turned to me. "Come on lil man yo rolling wit me."

Ruthann, Rhonda, and my Mama was quiet. They didn't say nothing to him. He laid down the law.

David was my Mama's pimp for a year then one day he was found dead slumped over in his Cadillac. The crazy thing is, the police found a brief case with $50,000 laying on the passenger seat next to him.

156

CHAPTER 40

Amaya

"Mommy! Mommy!"

I was sitting on my bed crying my eyes out when Amir ran into my room.

"Amir go back to bed."

"Amaya is throwing up!" he cried.

I was not in the mood for Amir and Amaya. Eric had just laid hands on me. I went into Amaya's bedroom and picked her up. Her little body was blazing hot and she was turning blue.

Five hours later, the emergency room doctors showed up in the waiting room to deliver the news that Amaya was breathing, her temperature went down, but she had a seizure. My heart dropped. I called Bridgette and she rushed up to the hospital. Once Amaya was stable, she took Amir home with her. I stayed at the hospital.

Amaya slept in the hospital crib and I sat in the chair next to her bed. I reached for the phone to page Eric but something stopped me. Then I ended up falling to my knees and I cried my soul out. The next day Bridgette and her Grandma came to visit. They convinced me to go home, change clothes, and rest. As soon as I got home, I paged Eric. He called me back ASAP.

"So you paging me to make up fo yo fuck up the other night?" he asked all arrogant.

"No Eric! I have to tell you…

"You owe me an apology, girl."

"Don't nobody put they hands on me."

"Call me back when you get it right, April."

"Amaya in the hospital Eric, she had a seizure last night!"

"What?"

"She's at Children's Hospital you coming up right?"

"My wife on her way home."

"So! Our daughter is the hospital, you need------

"Don't tell me what I need, you don't run shit, April!"

"Are you coming to see your daughter or what?"

"You her Mama, you got that."

"Don't call me no more Eric. You a tired ass nigga." I slammed the phone down. I cried myself to sleep. He never called me back.

Two days later Amaya was released from the hospital. After I put both of my kids to bed that night, I got on my knees and I prayed. I made a promise to God that I would never see, call, or think about Eric if Amaya could be healthy again.

A year later, finally moved out of my grandmother's house and into a four bedroom house in Blackjack. My grandmother's house sold for $275,000. My new job was lovely. I was hired as an executive secretary at Edward Jones. They let me work from home sometimes. It had been a year since I saw Eric. We lost touch and I was happy that he was out of my life.

CHAPTER 41

The Clinic

"Shyienne Johnson?" the nurse called me up to the counter. I made an appointment at the clinic because my vagina had been irritated and itchy for the past three days. It was March 1998.

After I gave the nurse my information, she told me to sit in the waiting area. I noticed two girls sitting together, one of the girls was short like me and she looked to be eight months pregnant. The girl sitting next to her was wearing a cute high ponytail. The Price is Right was playing on the mounted TV.

My ears perked up when I heard the pregnant girl say, "I'm tired of Eric not showing up to my appointments."

"What kind a car he driving? Maybe he bout to pull up?"

"Girl he drive a blue Regal." The pregnant girl fumed.

"Let me go out here and check. Be right back." Ponytail jumped up.

I sat next to the pregnant girl. "Excuse me?"

She turned toward me. "Did you say you was waiting on Eric?" I asked her.

"Yeah you know him?" she asked.

"I think we talking about the same dude." I confessed.

"How you know Eric?" She frowned.

I reached into my purse and pulled out my wallet. I showed her a picture of me and Eric.

"That's my baby's daddy!" she squealed.

"Eric is my husband." I shot back.

The nurse appeared. "Tiffany Brown?"

"That's me." She said. "You got some paper and a pen?"

I pulled out a Shopping Save receipt from my purse and borrowed a pen from the nurse. She rattled off her number then followed the nurse to the exam room.

I called Tiffany that evening. We agreed to meet up at her house the next day. For some reason when Eric made it home that night, I didn't mention Tiffany to him.

He handed me a book of eighty dollars in Food Stamps.

The next day I visited Tiffany. She lived in a studio apartment near downtown St. Louis.

"This is my first baby. I just turned eighteen a month ago." She confessed to me.

"You and Eric don't have kids?" she asked.

"Nah I can't make em." I confided.

"Aw sorry bout that. You so nice. I like you. Please don't tell Eric but he stole my Food Stamps the other day. And sometimes he..he.. hits me." She cried.

"Tiffany Eric gave me your Food Stamps." I confessed. Then I reached into my purse and pulled them out. "Here take em back." I handed them to her.

"Thank you!" she said then she hugged me. "I'm moving with my Auntie until I get section 8. I can't pay the rent here."

"Gimme your Auntie's phone number and address. I want us to be friends. If Eric comes around don't tell him I came over or that we met." I begged her.

A week later the phone bill came. Every time I opened a utility bill my stomach churned. The balance was $218. My eyes got big. I started reading over the statement and I noticed collect calls from Missouri Department of Corrections. Eric's gangsta friends from GTO was calling collect. At the bottom of the statement I spotted a local number that Eric called over twenty times. Curious I dialed the number. A female answered.

"Hello I found this number on my bill, do you know Eric?" I got straight to it.

"Hell yeah I know Eric. Who the fuck is this?" this girl had a girly voice but her tone was street.

"This his wife." I didn't yell. I stayed calm.

"Aw...I know about you. Eric is a grimy ass nigga. He ain't been to see the twins since I knocked him over the head with 40 ounce bottle. Don't no nigga put hands on me."

"Twins?" I was choked up.

"I got twin boys by him Taron and Laron." She announced. "He better keep his ass away from me tell him that."

"He don't know I'm talking to you. Whas yo name?" I asked her afraid that she might hang up on me.

"Brittany. What's yours?"

"Shay. Can we meet, Brittany?"

"I'm cool with that. You don't have to waste yo gas. I'll tell you everythang. I don't give a fuck about Eric."

That evening I drove to Brittany's house. She lived in an old three story red brick house on Page and Kingshighway Avenue. Teenagers were sitting on the steps grooving to rap music that was blasting from a boom box posted up in an open window.

"Is Brittany here?" I asked one of the overgrown teenage boys.

"Yeah wait here."

A few seconds later Brittany appeared at the front door. She was caramel brown with thick braids in her hair. She sported large gold hoop earrings.

She pointed her long fluorescent orange fingernail at me, "You Shay?"

"Yeah I'm Shay." I answered.

"Girl come on in. Y'all niggas move out the way. We got company."

I followed her down a long hallway and we passed up five different rooms. Each room had a group of people partying, talking loud, and blasting music. The smell of candied yams, cinnamon, and smoke meat made my stomach growl.

She stopped at the kitchen. It was people sitting down at the kitchen table playing cards. "You want some food. My Granny can burn."

"Girl yeah that sound good." I smiled remembering that I hadn't eaten all day.

"Here baby have a seat." An older lady wearing a flower gown patted to an empty chair.

"Here you go." Brittany sat a plate of food down in front of me. It was turkey, dressing, mac and cheese, and greens.

"Thank you, Brittany."

"Girl don't trip. Tell me why you here?" she asked.

I met Eric and Brittany's twin boys Laron and Taron. She even told me that she used to hustle for GTO and that's how her and Eric met. When I got home the apartment was empty. I was relieved that Eric didn't make it home yet.

The next day I went to see Monica. The pregnant girl who knocked on my door with her family in the middle of the night.

"Who is it?" a male voice answered her door.

"Shay. Is Monica home?"

The front door opened immediately.

"Who the fuck are-------

I noticed the skinny light skinned dude, Monica's brother.

"I'm Eric's wife."

"I know who you is. What the fuck you want wit my sister?"

"I just wanna talk. I have money for the baby."

He opened the door and yelled into the apartment, "Monie get in here. Somebody here to see you."

Monica appeared at the door holding her crying baby.

"Here." I handed her the money. "It's for the baby." Then I turned towards the staircase to leave.

"Hey, why you giving me this, did Eric send you over here?" she asked.

"Please don't tell Eric I was here." I begged her.

"What's yo name?" she asked.

"Shay. Promise me you won't----

"Girl I ain't seen Eric since I told him I was pregnant. He don't come around here."

"It's not much but I will get you more whenever I can."

"Come in, I want you to meet my Mama." She smiled.

I visited with Monica's family and she gave me her number. She even put her baby in my arms.

CHAPTER 42

Busted

"I'm on my way to see my kids, girl so don't trip when I get there."

I was chilling at Chance's crib.

"You ain't coming to see shit unless you got some money Eric."

"Have them ready when I get there." I wasn't tryin' to see no damn kids. My motive was to get Brittany's clothes off. April was on some stupid shit. Tryin' to get me to be her man. I wasn't havin' it. So I dipped on her ass.

"Don't step on my block Eric."

"I step where evah the --------

"If you roll up to my door. I'ma call yo wife. Aw yeah nigga she was over here and she know about yo ass."

"Stop lyin, my wife ain't been to yo house."

"Don't she drive a red Corolla nigga? If I was her I woulda put yo ass out."

I disconnected the call and started was pacing the living room.

"What's yo malfunction fool?" Chance asked me.

"Man I gotta go handle something. I holla at you later, my nig."

"Peace out!" he slapped me five.

My mind couldn't shake the news Brittany told me. I had to do something because losing Shay all over `again was gon break me.

CHAPTER 43

Red Hoodie

"Shay, Baby come ride wit me?"

"Eric I'm tired I just wanna chill tonight. It's my last day off." It was a Saturday evening and I was trying to rest because my shift at the nursing home started at 6am the next morning.

"Come on baby I'ma go get this weed and we be right back."

I threw on some sweats. It was at the end of March 1998. It had been a month since I met Tiffany and Brittany. They kept their promise and didn't tell Eric about me visiting them.

We hopped in the Regal and Eric rolled down to Tucker and Cass Avenue. He parked the Regal at the corner and kept the ignition going. A few minutes later, I noticed a flash of red out the corner of my eye. I turned around and spotted a tall lanky dude wearing a red hoodie running towards the car firing his gun. He shot at the car window and the glass shattered all over me.

I screamed, "Eric! Get us outtah here!" Eric sat there starring at the dude. Then I felt metal tearing into my flesh. I reached for Eric, and I tried to scream but blood started gushing out of my mouth like a water fountain. Even though I held my arms out to him, he pushed me away then I fell into darkness.

CHAPTER 44

We Still Family

“April you need to get here! Shay been shot five times! The doctors don't think she gon make it!” Ricky Shay's brother called me.

The cordless phone slipped from my hand. Everything else in between was a blur. Speeding through red lights, car horns honking, I didn't care, tears burning, blinding me. How did this happen? Please don't let her be dead! My legs wobbled when I stepped into the ice cold intensive care unit. She was lying in the hospital bed bandaged like a mummy. I slowed down as I moved closer to the hospital bed. On the verge of gagging from the stench of rubbing alcohol and hospital antiseptic, I held my breath. The plastic tubes and IV lines reminded me of white snakes. Beep! Beep! The hum of the machines made everything real. She looked like she was in a deep sleep. Stethoscopes, scrubs, and rapid fire conversations increased my devastation.

I called Bridgette once I arrived at the ICU. Ricky and his wife Toni was there. When Bridgette arrived, the first thing she asked was, "Where is Eric?" Everybody was in the waiting room area teary eyed and nervous. We could still see Shay's room from where we stood.

"He was here for a minute. After they examined him, the police came to question him." Ricky answered.

"Was he shot too?" Me and Bridgette asked at the same time.

"He was grazed." Ricky said.

"I bet you it was that GTO gang shit." Bridgette said.

All of a sudden a group of nurses and doctors started rushing to Shay's room. One of the nurses was pulling a cart and rolled it into the room.

"She must be crashing. Baby what if she don't make it?" Toni was crying.

"Baby she ain't gon come back from this. Shay is gon."
Ricky sobbed.

CHAPTER 45

The Job

I met Shank at a vacant house on St. Louis Ave.

"What up Eric? You got that bread. I gotta bounce. Met up with my girl cuz I'm tryin' get knee deep. Know what I'm sayin?"

"Ain't no what up fool."

"Man what you mean?" Shank looked at me crazy.

"I told yo ass to blast until she was dead."

"Nigga she look dead to me. Hand over that green."

I pulled out my glock and fired two shots to his forehead. He dropped onto the dusty hardwood floor. When I heard dogs barking, I dipped and ran ten blocks.

I hopped in my Regal and drove to the apartment. One block away, I saw red police lights flashing. It was ten cop cars posted in front of our apartment building. I busted a U turn.

Pulling over to a pay phone I page Chance. He called me back.

"I need to lay low, I can't come to yo house right now I'm hot."

"Meet me at the old trap house on Greer Ave." Chance said.

"Tell me what went down. We need to get at some fools or what?" Chance asked me. We was at the old trap house. It was vacant but Chance still had the keys.

"They tryin' to say that I had something to do with my wife getting' shot, man. I need to get outta town for real."

"You know who coulda blasted at you?"

"Man I don't know. I need to lay low so I could find out who done it."

"I think I got something. You stay here tonight. Don't leave until I get back at you. Stay outta sight." He said then bounced. I was so scared I was shaking. Chance was my only connect.

CHAPTER 46

Whisper

I jumped up ready to blast my gun when I heard the door open. It was Chance and three other people. My heart racing but thankful it wasn't the police.

I stood up when I noticed a cocoa brown honey wearing bronze eyeshadow, gold lipstick, a black short length fur coat, and four inch black heels on her feet.

"Eric this Danny G's wife, Whisper!" she had two body guards that stood at 6'5. Both of em look like WWE wrestlers. Danny G was the boss of GTO, but he was doing Federal time.

"How you doing?" I bowed. She didn't smile.

"You need to go underground?"

"Yeah I got some heat--------

"Nigga I don't give a fuck about yo backstory." Then she turned to Chance. "Did you tell him about the job?"

"I was checkin' to see if it was still on the table boss lady." Chance explained. This fool was givin' her mad respect. I wanted to break every bone in the bitch's face for walking in the house on her high horse.

"You gon be running packages and cooking in the kitchen." She glared at me running down the job.

"I'm cool wit that." I mumbled.

"You gettin' new papers too. So forget who you was nigga. If you get pulled over, you don't say shit. You call the number we give you. If you slip up yo gon be floatin in the Mississsppi."

"I feel you." I answered.

"Chance bring his ass to the spot in an hour."

"I got you boss lady!" Chance said all obedient.

Like clockwork, Chance took me to the spot. It was an old warehouse located on Laclede's Landing. On the outside, the building appeared to be vacant. The operation was in the basement of the warehouse. They made me strip out of my clothes. Next they handed me new clothes, a driver's license with a fake name, and car insurance paperwork. Excited I was planning on skipping out on them as soon as I could make it across state lines.

"I'm out!" Chance said slapping me five.

"Good lookin' out, my nig."

"I'ma catch up wit you." He said then dipped.

Whisper stepped up to me, her bodyguards a few feet behind her. A 9 MM glock was tucked into her holster on her waist. "Nigga you on the run?" she put her hand on her glock. Her hair flowing whenever she moved her head.

"Yeah...boss lady? I just need to lay low until I can figure some shit out!" She had me nervous.

"We putting you in the kitchen. Can't have you on the street bringing heat. Hand me them papers."

I handed her the papers exhaling glad that she didn't blow my head off but disappointed at the same time that I couldn't get outta dodge.

"Hard Rock?" she yelled to one of her bodyguards.

"What up, Queen?"

"Take him to the kitchen." Then she walked away.

"Let's roll." Hard Rock ordered me.

I ended up working in a gigantic lab in the basement of another warehouse they had in East St. Louis, Illinois, unpacking kilos for sixteen hours a day.

To Be Continued....

www.ingramcontent.com/pod-product-compliance
Lightning Source LLC
Chambersburg PA
CBHW071416150726
48000CB00001B/353